Goldilocks and the Wolf

Crabtree Publishing Company
www.crabtreebooks.com
1-800-387-7650

PMB 59051, 350 Fifth Ave.
59th Floor,
New York, NY 10118

616 Welland Ave.
St. Catharines, ON
L2M 5V6

Published by Crabtree Publishing in 2013

For Lynda and Charles

Series editor: Louise John
Editors: Katie Powell, Kathy Middleton
Notes to adults: Reagan Miller
Cover design: Paul Cherrill
Design: D.R.ink
Consultant: Shirley Bickler
Production coordinator and
   Prepress technician: Margaret Amy Salter
Print coordinator: Katherine Berti

Text © Hilary Robinson 2008
Illustration © Simona Sanfilippo 2008

First published in
2008 by Wayland
(A division of Hachette
Children's Books)

Printed in Hong Kong/
092012/BK20120629

Library and Archives Canada
Cataloguing in Publication

CIP available at Library and Archives Canada

Library of Congress
Cataloging-in-Publication Data

CIP available at Library of Congress

Goldilocks and the Wolf

Written by Hilary Robinson
Illustrated by Simona Sanfilippo

Crabtree Publishing Company
www.crabtreebooks.com

Goldilocks ran from the Three Bears' house, down into Bluebell Wood.

She stopped to rest beside a stream and saw Little Red Riding Hood.

Goldilocks told her the story
of the bears she had met that day...

Of how she had tried their porridge...

...and why she had run away.

Red Riding Hood said, "Are you feeling hungry? Would you like a bun?"

But as she laid the blanket down,
Goldilocks screamed, "Run!"

A wolf sat down between them
and said, "Buns! How kind of you!"

But the girls knew if they stayed there, he'd try to eat THEM, too!

11

"Quick, run!" said Goldilocks again,
and both girls turned quite pale.

They went to hide behind a bush,
but they spied the wolf's brown tail!

They ran and hid beside the pond.

Then Goldilocks gave a cry!

For peeking over the top of the reeds was the wild wolf's winking eye!

"I know," said Goldilocks.
"Let's hide over here."

But over by the gate they saw
the wolf's brown pointed ear!

"Let's go!" they cried. "The riverbank has trees to hide beneath!"

But peeking through the rustling leaves
they saw the wolf's sharp teeth!

Goldilocks said, "Follow me!
We'll race towards that farm."

"We'll try to find the Three Bears there and sound the wolf alarm!"

21

"Listen," said Red Riding Hood,
"I've got a good idea."

"Let's go to my Grandmother's house.
She lives really very near."

But, as they ran, they heard a howl
that echoed through the trees,
and when they turned around they
saw the wolf down on his knees.

"Don't go," he sobbed.
"Oh, please don't go.
Don't leave me all alone."

"No one wants to be my friend.
I'm always on my own!

"I'm just a friendly, gentle wolf.
I'm really very meek."

"And all I want to play with you
is a game of..."

"...HIDE and SEEK!"

Notes for adults

Tadpoles: Fairytale Jumbles are designed for transitional and early fluent readers. The books may also be used for read-alouds or shared reading with younger children.

Tadpoles: Fairytale Jumbles are humorous stories with a unique twist on traditional fairy tales. Each story can be compared to the original fairy tale, or appreciated on its own. Fairy tales are a key type of literary text found in the Common Core State Standards

THE FOLLOWING BEFORE, DURING, AND AFTER READING SUGGESTIONS SUPPORT LITERACY SKILL DEVELOPMENT AND CAN ENRICH SHARED READING EXPERIENCES:

1. Make reading fun! Choose a time to read when you and the child are relaxed and have time to share the story.

2. Before reading, invite the child to preview the book. The child can read the title, look at the illustrations, skim through the text, and make predictions as to what will happen in the story. Predicting sets a clear purpose for reading and learning.

3. During reading, encourage the child to monitor his or her understanding by asking questions to draw conclusions, making connections, and using context clues to understand unfamiliar words.

4. After reading, ask the child to review his or her predictions. Were they correct? Discuss different parts of the story, including main characters, setting, main events, the problem and solution. If the child is familiar with the original fairy tale, invite he or she to identify the similarities and differences between the two versions of the story.

5. Encourage the child to use his or her imagination to create fairytale jumbles based on other familiar stories.

6. Give praise! Children learn best in a positive environment.

IF YOU ENJOYED THIS BOOK, WHY NOT TRY ANOTHER TADPOLES: FAIRYTALE JUMBLES STORY?

Snow White and the Enormous Turnip	*978-0-7787-8024-3 RLB*	*978-0-7787-8035-9 PB*
The Elves and the Emperor	*978-0-7787-8025-0 RLB*	*978-0-7787-8036-6 PB*
Three Pigs and a Gingerbread Man	*978-0-7787-8026-7 RLB*	*978-0-7787-8037-3 PB*

VISIT WWW.CRABTREEBOOKS.COM FOR OTHER CRABTREE BOOKS.